SPACE CRUISE 2069

Alan Chambers

Table of Contents

Thanks to my friends and family, who have given me support and positive feedback after reading 'Space Cruise 2069' and have encouraged me to have it published.

About The Author

Alan Chambers was born in Edinburgh in 1944, where he has lived his entire life. He wanted to join the Royal navy at 15, but as his mother refused to sign the consent papers, he took an apprenticeship in a local engineering company. He still wanted to go to sea, though, and joined the Royal Naval Reserve at 17 years of age as a junior stoker. He continued to serve for a total of 30 years, and during this time, he was promoted several times to achieve the rank or rate of Chief Marine Engineering Artificer or CMEA. This qualified him to take charge of the engineering department onboard mine counter-measures ships of the Royal Navy. After serving 25 years, he was presented to HRH Princess Anne to be awarded a bar for his long service medal.

His hobbies are hill walking, bowls and short story writing. He was inspired to write 'Space Cruise 2069' during the COVID lockdown.

Introduction

'SPACE CRUISE 2069' A futuristic passenger space adventure to Mars with fast exciting excursions to detailed actual places and features on the 'Red Planet'. During this space cruise the passengers and crew suffer some scary mishaps which turns out to be life changing for all of them.

Part 1

"Good morning everyone. This is your captain Mike Morgan speaking. May I take this opportunity to welcome you on board this Galaxy spacecraft which is about to begin her maiden passenger voyage to the planet Mars. Incidentally, and for your information, this is in celebration of it being exactly one hundred years since man first walked on the moon.

This particular voyage has been made possible with the benefit of the latest technological advancements, including hybrid engines using a combination of conventional and nuclear fuels. You have all completed the suitability induction course, but just to refresh your memories, I'll again explain what's about to happen next. We will be lifting off in a few minutes from now, using conventional fuel to get us into orbit. Initially after lift-off, you will experience strong G-forces. However, with our revolutionary design in space seats, this should feel no worse than a ride on a big dipper at a fairground. Your slight discomfort will last for several minutes until we are free from the Earth's gravitational pull, and from thereon, you will experience the somewhat more pleasant sensation of weightlessness.

"After a few times around the world for a photo shoot, we'll rendezvous and dock with the recently completed advanced international space station. While we're there, we will be embarking on nuclear fuel rods to enable us to continue the next leg of our journey powered with a blast from nuclear fission. This work will take about four hours to complete, and as the station provides its own artificial gravity, you will be able to disembark and enjoy seeing some of its amazing features. Now sit back and enjoy the ride.

"Ten seconds to lift off", announced an electronic voice. "10, 9, 8, 7, 6, 5, 4, 3, 2, 1, CONTACT".

The giant rocket engine roared into life, enabling the largest delta-winged spacecraft ever built to rise from the earth's surface.

Bill and Sandra Mclean, who were seated near the front of the passenger cabin, were thrown back into their seats as the ship began to accelerate. "Here we go Sandra", shouted Bill over the engine's noise. "It's too late to change your mind now".

Sandra shouted back, "You don't have to worry about me, because I'm really looking forward to this". It took about five minutes for the craft to exit the earth's atmosphere with its gravitational pull and for the sensation of weightlessness to kick in. This caused a bit of excitement with some hilarity from the twenty-four passengers. "Ladies and gentlemen", announced the captain, "I hope the launch was not too uncomfortable for you. However, you will be glad to know that since the worst part is over, you can now enjoy the spectacular views of our mother Earth. If you look out of your personal observation ports, you should be able to see the complete outline of Australia and New Zealand with the South Pole in the distance.

We will orbit the earth three times, adjusting our flight path as we go, until we are in a position for a rendezvous with the space station".

"Bill, this is simply wonderful", remarked Sandra. "Weren't we so lucky to have won this trip in that competition you entered".

Bill replied, "Yes, we sure were, and just think, this is something we'll remember all our lives".

Sitting in seats directly behind them were Jim and Margaret Ross. They had decided on this once-in-a-lifetime trip because Margaret had not long ago been diagnosed with terminal cancer. It was Jim's idea to sell up his business and spend the money on something quite out of the ordinary that she might be able to appreciate. "Thank you Jim, for being so thoughtful", said Margaret. "I'm really looking forward to this, and to think that we are about to embark on a voyage that millions of ordinary folks will never be able to afford."

Jim took her hand in his and replied with a breaking voice. "I don't care about the money because it's the least I could do for you, especially after what you have been going through".

"Come on now", she lightly scolded. "You promised me that we wouldn't dwell on my illness. Remember this, I couldn't ask for a better last vacation".

She looked at the handheld body scanning device that had been loaned to her by the hospital, and could see that the cancer was still evident and growing, confirming that she may not have long to live once this adventure is over. Each one of the other passengers had their own reasons for coming on this journey.

Directly across from Jim and Margaret sat a young honeymoon couple who had been given this treat as a wedding gift from their wealthy parents. The other passengers were a mixture of different nationalities, some of whom were from Middle Eastern and Asian royal families.

It was clear that most of the travellers were from rich or privileged backgrounds. After orbiting the earth three times, the space station came into view, and the sheer size of it was breathtaking, for it looked like a gigantic black tubular wheel revolving around a central axle. They could see dozens of lights from its accommodation and observation windows. The ship edged slowly closer until it found a bump, to which it locked automatically into a docking port. "Welcome to the international space station", announced the captain. "As I said earlier, feel free to disembark while we prepare for the continuance of our journey. For those passengers who may be interested, I have arranged a tour of the facilities for you. I can now confidently tell you that anyone going on this tour will surely find it fascinating. Therefore, it's regarded as a must-see."

All the passengers took the opportunity of disembarking the craft and going on the tour. They found the artificial gravity strange at first, because it made one feel slightly lighter than normal. After a short unsteady walk through an adjoining concourse, they boarded one of four open-topped electric vehicles and moved off in convoy. It was like travelling along a wide brightly-lit tunnel, constantly bending and without an end. There were passages leading off to different facilities at regular intervals along the way. The guide explained that since there were over 4,000 people working and living on the space station, it was necessary to have their own hospital, police, and fire services. They visited accommodation, recreational, and research areas.

However, the main and largest facility, by far, was the control centre, being manned by hundreds of personnel around the clock. These people were split into different groups having various responsibilities. One group was controlling any spacecraft coming or going within an area of millions of square miles. A second group was to monitor and divert any meteorites that could be considered a danger to the space station or, indeed, the earth itself. A third group had the more clandestine task of spying on some of the unstable third-world countries, and hence keeping the world's leading authorities informed of any likely terrorist activities that might be about to happen. All seemed to work exceptionally well and was very impressive. At the end of the tour, they were treated to lunch in one of the restaurants, which they were able to enjoy without the restrictions of weightlessness.

Once back onboard the spacecraft, the captain's voice came over the broadcast. "Fellow astronauts, I hope you enjoyed your visit to the space station, and that you were properly looked after by the staff during the tour. If you are anything like me, you will be feeling proud of the achievements of the world's leading nations in the making of this fantastic complex. The cabin crew will be coming 'round shortly to make sure you are properly strapped in for our blast-off. Although it's true that we are weightless, the initial acceleration may cause you to float around too much. While that is being done, I will explain to you what is going to happen from here on. With the benefit of a controlled nuclear blast, we will be propelled at the fantastic speed of around 400,000 miles an hour towards an area where we will meet up with the planet Mars in her orbit path of the Sun. To let you understand, Mars, at this time, is relatively close to Earth at about fifty-eight million miles, and as we will be travelling just short of ten million miles a day, we would expect to be there in six days. After we get underway, our leading cabin crew member will tell you more about the facilities we have on board to help with our journey.”

“Standby for blast off”, announced the electronic voice. “10, 9, 8, 7, 6, 5, 4, 3, 2, 1, CONTACT'.”

There was a muffled explosion from the rear of the craft, and the ship sped away from the space station at a fantastic speed. On monitor screens above their heads, they could see the space station and Earth dropping away fast. Looking out of their personal observation ports, they saw what looked like shooting stars moving across their line of vision. This, of course, was an illusion brought on by the effects of the speed they were travelling at.

"Fellow space travellers", announced the leading cabin crew member. "My name is Joe Mathews; me and my staff will be taking care of you during the journey. We will replenish your space rations when required, and all you have to do when you are in need of anything is to call us up using the green button on your armrest. As demonstrated during your induction training, we have onboard, special weightless, adapted washrooms. When you feel the need to make use of this facility, please contact a crew member. As this journey will last six days, you are required by law to do mandatory exercises to prevent muscle wastage brought on by the prolonged effects of weightlessness. Passengers will be requested to leave their seats four at a time and go into an exercise area twice daily. There, under instruction, you will do thirty minutes of space aerobics, which, although quite rigorous, should still be fun. There will also be a variety of entertainment programs, both live and on your monitor's screens, to help relieve boredom.

After you have been awake for twelve hours, we will dim the cabin lights and introduce a safe sleeping gas into the air conditioning system. This will put you into a pleasant sleep for a period of twelve hours. With the effect of weightlessness, you will be guaranteed to have a very comfortable night and wake up feeling completely refreshed".

With the benefit of space aerobics and entertainment programs, the waking time each day passed quickly enough. Each morning when they awoke, there was an image of Mars on their monitor screens. The size of it on the second day appeared to be about that of a ping pong ball, and it grew steadily each morning until, on the fifth day, it looked like a giant red-marbled weather balloon. On the sixth day, they were awakened with a few bars of the classical musical theme to 'Mars the God of War' being played over the broadcast. When the music stopped, Captain Morgan cheerfully announced, "Good morning, space travellers. You'll be pleased to know that we have arrived, and I would just like to say, welcome to the 'Red Planet.' We will shortly be going into orbit, where you will all get an opportunity to descend to within 500 feet from the surface in one of our two shuttle crafts. These crafts can take six passengers at a time for a flying tour. Although we are unable to land, I can guarantee you all a magical flight lasting about four hours. For those passengers still onboard, either waiting to go on the next tour or having returned from the last one, you will not be bored, because I will be adjusting our orbit path frequently to allow you to see as much of the planet as possible".

The spacecraft slowed down, adjusted its trajectory, and slipped into orbit. They could make out mountains, valleys, and what looked like dried-out riverbeds. There were vast areas of flat desert where one could have imagined a sea might have been at one time. The poles at either end seemed to have a light dusting of what looked like frost.

"If you look out of your windows now", announced the captain, "you will be able to see the famous face on Mars as was discovered in 1976 by Viking One. At that time, it caused a bit of a stir because it looked like some kind of monument, but alas, on further investigation, it turned out to be nothing more than a natural feature".

"Oh yes, I can see it", remarked Margaret Ross. "Look Jim, doesn't it look weird".

Jim stretched across to see for himself. "It sure does", he agreed, "for it's almost as if it were man-made".

"May I have your attention", announced Joe Mathews. "We will shortly be boarding the shuttle crafts for the first flying tour of the surface. Will the following passengers please come through to the exercise area where you will each be briefed and kitted out with your protective space suits? Bill and Sandra Mclean, Jim and Margaret Ross, Ian and Catlin Wells, who happen to be our newlyweds". There was an immediate applause accompanied by a few light-hearted cat-calls.

"Please come forward two at a time in the order that your names were called". Bill and Sandra unbuckled their seat restraints, floated off, and pulled their way along the cabin and out through the access hatch into the exercise area. Two of the crew members were waiting to assist them with putting on their space suits. Once they were securely kitted up, they were briefed about their use, then led down through another hatch into what looked like a bomb bay where two small space shuttles were locked into cradles side by side. There they were directed through an entrance door of the nearest shuttle craft and ushered to a seating position with a large observation window. One of the crew members strapped them in tightly and put on their space helmets. These helmets would provide them with an air supply, and being made of a clear transparent material, gave them unrestricted all-round vision. Within their helmets were microphones and receivers so that they could hear and talk to each other during the flight.

Once the other passengers had been seated, a voice broke into their receivers, "Hello folks, this is your pilot and guide talking. My name is Neil. I would just like to take a few minutes to explain to you what is about to happen. The bomb bay doors will open, and the cradle will release the craft, allowing us to drop away gently from the mother ship. Once we are clear, our engine will fire up, adjusting our angle to give us a safe trajectory to enter Mars's atmosphere. We will then drift down using Mars's gravitational pull while controlling our speed with reverse thrusts of the engine. This manoeuvre will continue until we are about 500 feet from the surface. At that point, the engine will take over completely, controlling our flight for the rest of the trip. We will be travelling at speeds of up to 900 miles an hour and will be able to drop as low as 200 feet in places. I will be pointing out areas of interest during the flight, but if you have any questions, please don't hesitate to ask. Now enjoy the tour, and we should be home in time for tea".

There was a whirring sound as the bomb bay doors opened, and a metallic clunk as the cradle released the shuttlecraft. Through their windows, it appeared like they were going down in a glass elevator as the craft started to slowly drop out through the doors. Once clear, they could squint up and see the mother ship above them pulling away. The engine fired into life, and the craft tilted towards the surface. There was a bit of turbulence as it entered the planet's atmosphere, and they started to feel the onset of gravity again. The craft continued to descend, being intermittently slowed down by the reverse thrust of the engine. Each time this happened, they were being thrown forward against their seat restraints. After a few minutes, Neil, the pilot, announced that they were now at a height of 500 feet. The cabin was filled with a red glow caused by the reflection from the surface as they skimmed swiftly over a vast arid plain. Neil's voice broke in again. "Please don't be disappointed by the views at the moment, because we are just about to enter the Valles Marineris, named after the Mariner spacecraft, which was the first to photograph it up close in 1971. This is a fault that stretches for 2,500 miles and is 120 miles wide in places by 4 miles deep, which incidentally is the largest valley in the entire solar system and four times the depth of the Grand Canyon. I will manoeuvre the craft down into the canyon and fly along its length at a height of 200 feet from its base".

The canyon appeared beneath them, and they felt the craft tilt as it descended into it. Both sides of the valley rose high on either side of the craft as it dropped further down. It certainly was exciting, if not a little scary, for it was like entering the jaws of hell, and it definitely put the Grand Canyon into the shade for sightseeing. They banked and weaved their way along the bottom of the valley for two hours, giving the passengers the most thrilling ride of their lives before having to rise out and above the arid plain again. Neil's voice broke into their helmets, "Well, did you all enjoy that?" There were shouts of approval from all six of the passengers. "We are now going to visit another feature before returning to the mother ship. We will be flying over and around a volcano called the Olympic Mons. Don't worry though, because it became inactive a very long time ago. However, it is so large, being 370 miles in diameter and 16 miles high, which I will add, is the highest mountain in the entire solar system, and four times the height of Everest. I'm sure you're going to be impressed even more, so here we go". The craft banked and sped away at right angles to the valley.

Within a short space of time, there appeared on the horizon a mountainous region. The craft increased its height and flew directly over a giant crater stretching into the distance. Suddenly, and to everyone's alarm, the craft started to jerk violently. Then it involuntarily began to lose height, causing it to rapidly drop down into the crater itself. It was obvious the pilot was having difficulty controlling her, and he lowered the speed, fearing that they might run out of distance and hit the crater's wall at the far end. Finally, he had to make the decision to set the craft down on the base of the crater. Reducing the speed even more, he allowed her to coast gently to a safe spot, where she came to rest with a slight bump on her telescopic landing legs. The engine stopped, and there was utter silence apart from some whimpering coming from the direction of Catlin Wells. Neil's voice broke the silence. "As you can see, we have hit a bit of a snag. However, please don't be alarmed, because although it may look bad, we have allowed for such events. I have already radioed the mother ship, and she has instructed the other shuttle craft to return immediately with her passengers so that she can load up with engineers and equipment to enable her to come back and rescue us. In the meantime, while we are waiting, why not take a walk outside and enjoy the fresh air".

Bill McLean shouted, "Ha-ha! That's very funny".

"Seriously", replied Neil. "You can safely go outside for a short while with your space suits on, so long as we are shaded from the extreme rays of the sun, and being deep inside this crater, we should have nothing to worry about in that respect. Then at least you can brag that you have walked on the surface of Mars".

Margaret Ross spoke up, "Well, I don't know about you Jim, but I'm definitely going outside because I wouldn't miss this opportunity for the entire world or should I have said Mars". Jim responded, "If you're going outside, then you're not going without me". Sandra and Bill Mclean also announced that they wanted to take the opportunity, whereas the honeymooners sat holding onto each other, obviously upset with their predicament.

The outer door opened with a hiss, and a ladder lowered automatically from a compartment below. Neil came out from behind his controls and invited anyone wanting to go outside to come forward. All four of the willing passengers released their seat restraints, got up, and moved unsteadily towards the door. Neil showed them where they should hold onto while going down the few rungs to the surface. Bill Mclean volunteered to be the first to go and turned around to go down backwards, as was advised to do so by Neil. He slowly moved down one step at a time until he felt his feet touch the soft surface. "That was one small step for a man, and one giant leap for mankind," he said, amused at the thought that he had just repeated Neil Armstrong's first words when he had stepped onto the surface of the moon one hundred years before.

Margaret Ross's heart was thumping at the thought of joining Bill on the surface and went down the ladder assisted by Bill at the foot and Jim at the top. Sandra was next, followed finally by Jim, until all four were standing on the surface. It was like being in the middle of a giant red coloured soup bowl. Margaret looked up with awe at the beauty of the sky and couldn't help letting a tear form in her eye. On seeing this, Jim took her gloved hand in his and stood with her silently, as she gazed up at the heavens. Sandra tried to pick up a rock and fell over, to the amusement of Bill, who helped her back onto her feet again. "What on Earth, oh sorry, I should have said Mars, were you trying to do there?" he asked with a laugh.

"I only wanted a souvenir to take home", she replied. Margaret Ross pointed to the ground and spoke. "Jim, look at all the footprints we have made. Just think about it, these are the first prints man has ever made in this place, and they could be here forever. What a lasting legacy to our lives, don't you think?" Jim got a lump in his throat, and just nodded his agreement.

After about thirty minutes, Neil's voice broke into their helmets, "Time to come back inside children. The rescue craft is on its way". All four slowly made their way back inside the craft, and the door closed again. They sat, chattering excitedly about their walk on Mars, until they heard the noise of an engine far above them.

"You no doubt can hear the other craft", announced Neil. "He is circling us very slowly at about 1000 feet above the top of the volcano. Unfortunately, the pilot is unable to come any lower as he does not want to risk the chance of getting into the same difficulty. Therefore, I'll explain how they are going to rescue us. Quite simply, they are going to winch down a capsule which can take one person at a time and return with them to the safety of the rescue craft".

There were audible gasps from all around the cabin and sobbing coming from the direction of Catlin Wells. Bill Mclean piped up angrily. "How are they going to manage a stunt like that if they're circling us at a thousand feet and not even hovering?"

"Now please don't be alarmed", replied Neil. "This is no ordinary capsule as it is fitted with a gyroscope to keep it steady, and it will be laser guided to a spot right outside the door. To explain further, although the craft above us is indeed circling, albeit very slowly, there is a rotating device fitted 500 feet up on a titanium cable keeping the capsule perfectly still and vertical. Once we have someone safely inside the capsule, I will radio the rescue craft to start winching it up. The return journey will take about 10 minutes. Now, who volunteers to be the first?"

Margaret Ross immediately indicated that she would be perfectly willing to be the first to go. "Oh no you don't", interrupted Jim. "I'll be the first to go".

"Jim dear", she countered, "let me do this for the benefit of the others, so that they can see that there is nothing to be frightened of. After all, I have nothing to lose if anything did happen to go wrong".

"Oh, very well", he reluctantly agreed. "You always were a stubborn one. Off you go then, and I'll see you onboard the rescue craft".

An egg-shaped capsule appeared directly outside of the door, as was promised. There was a rotating cable attached to a complex swivel fitting on its roof and reaching up into the Martian sky. Neil took Margaret's arm and guided her out through the door of the craft and across the few paces to the capsule. He undid a hatch and opened it. Margaret climbed inside and strapped herself into a single seat. Neil closed the hatch securing it tightly. Inside, there was a courtesy light and a small porthole so that she could see something of what was happening. Neil stepped away and spoke into a handheld radio. The capsule immediately lifted off at a steady speed and disappeared into a dark Martian sky. Everyone left onboard sat in silence, waiting for the news that the first rescue had been a success.

Finally, after about ten minutes, Neil's voice broke into their helmets. "Here is the news you have all been waiting for. Margaret is safely onboard the rescue craft, and they are sending the capsule back down to pick up the next passenger. Now, if the gentlemen are in agreement, I would like to send one of the two remaining ladies first, and suggest that since she is obviously upset, it should be Catlin Wells". Everyone nodded in agreement.

The capsule returned, and Catlin was led outside by her husband and the pilot. At first, she refused to enter it, but after some cajoling by her husband, they managed to get her inside. Once there and closed up, the capsule lifted off again. This operation continued a further five times until all the passengers, including the pilot, were taken off.

Inside the rescue craft, there was a great sense of relief at being safe once more, as the craft banked away and increased its height rapidly. After several minutes, it rendezvoused and docked successfully with the mother ship. The passengers were escorted off in pairs to the exercise area, where they were assisted with the removal of their space suits.

Once everyone was back in their seats, the captain's voice came over the broadcast. "I do apologise sincerely for the mishap you encountered while on the flying tour. I'm sure it must have been quite an ordeal for you to have to land inside a volcanic crater. However, do try to look on the bright side, because you will be able to tell your grandchildren that you have walked on the surface of the planet Mars. You may be wondering about the shuttle craft that we have left behind. Well, a salvage craft will rescue it at a future date. In the meantime, I don't think it will be stolen or vandalized". There was a chuckle from the passengers at this dry remark. "In view of what has happened", he continued, "I'm going to put a suggestion to you. Do the remainder of the passengers, not having been on a flying tour yet, still wish to go on one now with the remaining shuttle, or would you prefer to cancel?" All of the remaining passengers voted to cancel the flying tour. "Very well then", said the captain, "let's prepare ourselves for our return journey".

"Ten seconds to blast off", announced the robotic voice. "10, 9, 8, 7, 6, 5, 4, 3, 2,1, CONTACT".

There was the familiar muffled explosion again, but this time the cabin immediately filled with a blinding white light for about ten seconds before returning to normal.

There were murmurs of concern at this strange event from all around the cabin. Rubbing her eyes, Margaret Ross turned to Jim and asked, "What you think has just happened dear?" Jim was also rubbing his eyes as he answered, "I'm sorry, but I haven't got the faintest idea. Perhaps the captain will be able to enlighten us".

Sandra McLean turned to her husband and said, "Bill, I don't know about you, but I feel slightly strange after that white light."

"Me too", he replied, "what do you suppose caused it?" A passenger from further back in the cabin shouted, "Can someone please tell us what has just happened, because I can't see properly".

Joe Mathews, the senior cabin crew member answered, "Please try to remain calm, the captain will make an announcement as soon as his investigations are complete". After a short while, the captain made a personal appearance inside the cabin. "I wanted to come in here in person and speak to all of you directly. Firstly, I can assure you that this spacecraft is still intact, and is in perfect working order. Therefore, we are progressing on our return journey as normal. After a thorough investigation by my engineers into the cause of the bright light, it appears that the engine's governor was too slow to kick in immediately after blasting off. As a result of that happening, it seems that for a period of ten seconds or so, we had been travelling at the speed of light. The upside to this is, we have shortened the time of our return journey. However, on the downside, we don't know for sure what lasting effect, if any, this may have on our bodies as no one has ever travelled at the speed of light before. As for myself, I feel great with no obvious side effects. Therefore, I don't think we will have anything to worry about on that score".

The remainder of the day was uneventful, and most people were glad when the lights were dimmed and the sleeping gas was introduced.

The following morning, Margaret Ross woke up before the lights came fully on and did the one thing she did every morning when she first awakened; she looked at the illuminated screen on her personal body scanner. She gave it a knock with the heel of her hand because it did not seem to be registering correctly. It showed that there was no cancer. She switched it off and then waited thirty seconds before switching it on again. Scanning in progress, it read, taking a few minutes to go through its cycle before finally settling and stating that the scanning was complete. To her utter amazement, it read that there was no cancer present. "Jim look", she cried. "Something strange and wonderful has happened to me". Jim glanced at the screen on her scanner and exclaimed in amazement, "Good Lord, so it seems, how can we account for that?" Just at that point, the cabin lights came fully on.

As they looked at each other, they couldn't believe their eyes, for they both appeared to be slightly younger. As the other passengers awoke, there were excited squeals, and loud voices as each one of them found that they, too, had become proportionately younger. The honeymooners who were closest to Jim and Margaret were looking puzzled at each other. A voice from the rear of the cabin shouted. "In heaven's name, what has just happened? Can someone please explain?" At that moment, a fresh-faced Captain Morgan entered the cabin. He stood and paused for a moment before speaking. "Fellow pioneers, he announced. I'm calling you this, because that is exactly what we have become. As you are all aware, we have experienced a change to our bodies whereby we appear to have become a little younger. To some of you, this may be quite alarming, but to others, it may be regarded as a blessing. Whatever way we look at it, this has happened, and we will have to accept it.

Unfortunately, that's not the end of our problems because I must give you some more news, both good and bad. The good news is that this spacecraft is functioning perfectly normally, and we're continuing on our journey back to Earth. The bad news is, and I don't quite know how to explain this to you, but here goes anyway. You may have noticed that I said that we are returning to Earth rather than the space station. This is because the space station isn't there. You'll no doubt be asking yourselves, what has happened to the space station? Well, to put it simply, it has not been built yet. You see, not only have our bodies become younger, but it appears that we have also gone back in time". There were audible gasps followed by mutterings from the four corners of the cabin. The captain raised his hand to call for quiet as he continued.

"How do I know we have gone back in time? Well earlier this morning, I tried but failed to make contact with the space station, but I did manage to contact the Earth instead. Their response, however, was a hostile one, stating that they have no record of any spaceship of our type and size being in this area. As a result of that, we are to be treated as a possible threat until we can prove otherwise. I tried explaining who we were and what had happened to us, but they still don't believe me. They told me that the new space station was still in the planning stage and not due for completion for several years. They also said that the date is 2059, and as you know, that is ten years ago. After pleading our innocence and begging for their help, they have reluctantly agreed to allow us to land at the old N.A.S.A. spaceport of Houston, Texas. However, when we do land, we will be met by the military and be treated as a threat until we have all been fully screened by the authorities. How was it possible for us to have gone back in time, you may well ask. I seem to remember when I attended school, the great mathematician Albert Einstein had a theory that if it were possible for a body to travel at the speed of light, it may also have an effect on time itself. It seems that his theory has been proven to be correct. Now the fact that we have travelled backwards through time, has caused, or rather, is going to be a bit of a problem for us, because this means that we ourselves have not actually left the Earth yet. For that reason alone, we don't know what lies ahead for each of us. When you think about it, does this mean that we have become different people, and as such, it's possible that we could end up meeting up with ourselves. This is a frightening concept which I'm sure will be as difficult for you as it is for me to come to terms with. We can only wait and see what happens when we do finally get home, if indeed we have homes to go to".

The ship arrived back at the location of the new international space station only to find that, as expected, it was not there. In its place was an old, abandoned space station. The captain made an announcement, "As you can see folks, we have arrived at an old space station. It is obsolete and unmanned, and therefore we're unable to dock with it, but I have been in radio contact with the Earth for our re-entry instructions. Alas, it seems that we are not out of the woods yet, because they will not allow us to land with nuclear fuel rods onboard". There were murmurs as the captain continued. "I understand that this must be upsetting for you. However, let me assure you that I will do everything in my power to resolve this issue. I am now going to have a meeting with my engineering staff to see if there's any way we can safely offload the fuel rods".

It was three hours later before the captain's voice was heard again. "Sorry to have kept you waiting folks, but I'm sure you will appreciate that since we're unable to dock with the space station, this has not been an easy problem for us to deal with. The good news is that we have now come up with a plan of action that has been discussed and approved by the authorities on Earth. Our engineers intend to encapsulate the fuel rods within the rescue capsule for safe removal and transfer to the shuttlecraft. The shuttlecraft will then depart unmanned as we are able to control it remotely. It will be guided over to the old station, where it will attach itself securely to it with a device fabricated by our engineers. The idea being that this device will latch and lock onto a suitable anchor point so that the craft can be tethered to the station using a length of titanium cable from the rescue gear. It all sounds simple enough but let me assure you that it's far from it. However, as we have simulated this manoeuvre several times, we are fairly confident that we can pull it off. If, on the other hand, we fail, then our alternative is that we will have to wait for about six weeks for a rescue craft to be launched from Earth. As soon as we're ready, I'll let you know so that you can observe this manoeuvre for yourselves".

A short time later, the captain's voice came on again. "Okay folks, we're ready to launch the shuttle craft, and you will be able to see a bit of what's happening through your observation ports. I'll also give you a running commentary as we go. If you look on your overhead monitors, you will see the craft is now descending from the mother ship".

The passengers watched the craft being lowered and its controls being tested. The captain spoke again, "You will have seen that we have a good control of the craft, so we're now going send it away towards the space station. Once there, we will laser guide the grabbing device to a desired anchor point on the station. Keep your fingers crossed because here we go". The craft could be seen clearly from Margaret Ross's observation port. "

Look Jim," she said, "there it goes heading towards the space station".

Jim replied, '"Yes, so I see. Here's hoping that it all goes according to plan, because I don't fancy sitting here for weeks on end waiting to be rescued".

The captain spoke again, "As the shuttle is nearing the space station, we will be searching for a suitable anchor point to attach her. If I do happen to go quiet during this time, don't worry because it'll be that I'm having to concentrate on the task at hand". On seeing the shuttle being manoeuvred around the space station, Margaret was sitting with her fingers crossed in one hand while holding on to Jim's with the other.

Finally, after what seemed an age, the captain's voice came on. "Passengers, I'm happy to report that after three attempts, we have successfully managed to securely attach the shuttle onto the space station. There were cheers followed by a round of applause before the captain continued speaking. "Since we have successfully overcome the problem of safely discarding the fuel rods, we can now make our preparations for our re-entry to our mother earth and home, that is, if we have homes to go to. Finally, I say this to you in all sincerity. May God be with us and take care of us in whatever kind of future we will have. Good luck everyone because here we go."

Part 2

Having safely re-entered the Earth's atmosphere, the spacecraft, with the benefit of its delta wings levelled out and then lowered an undercarriage in preparation for a horizontal landing. The captain slowed the craft down sufficiently to rendezvous with three fighter planes that had been sent to escort them. His voice came over the broadcast. "Passengers, if you look out of your ports, you will see that we are being escorted by three military aircraft but let me assure you, there's no need for alarm, as their sole purpose is to protect and guide us to our designated landing strip".

The craft banked to follow the fighter planes and commenced its descent. The ground was beginning to take shape, with various features becoming recognisable. Down they dropped until a landing strip came into view, and at that point, the fighter planes departed, leaving the captain to navigate the remainder of his descent on his own.

The landing strip came up fast to meet them, and there was a heavy bump when the wheels of the undercarriage finally touched down. They coasted along the runway for several miles before coming to a gradual and eventual stop. Being relieved to be safely back on the ground again, the passengers gave a cheer with a customary round of applause.

Looking out of her port window, Margaret Ross said, "Look Jim, at the welcoming reception they've laid on for us. Look at all of those vehicles lined up along the side of the runway". Jim stretched across to see for himself and replied, "I'm not so sure about it being a friendly reception though, because if you look again, you will see that they are all military vehicles that appear locked and loaded". There began the sounds of angry murmurs among the other passengers at seeing this display of power. On hearing this commotion, Joe Mathews, the leading cabin crew member, made an announcement, "Passengers, please try to remain calm until the captain comes through to talk to you".

Bill McLean turned to his wife and spoke with a voice loud enough for all to hear. "I don't much like the look or sound of this Sandra". She rebuked him by saying that he should wait until he hears what the captain has to say before jumping to his own conclusions. Other passengers were beginning to get agitated, until Joe Mathews made another announcement. "Please ladies and gentlemen, please be patient a little longer. The captain is having talks with the authorities as I speak, and when they are complete, he will come through and explain everything to you".

It was about thirty minutes later before the captain made his appearance, and it struck everyone that all was not well by the look on his face. He addressed the passengers. "The spokesperson I have been conferring with is a representative of the world's council of nations. She has instructed me to tell you that our story about us having travelled here through time has been rejected. As a result of that, we are to be kept under arrest until we can give them a proper explanation of where we have come from".

Bill McLean piped up, "How can we explain things any better than what you will have done yourself?"

The captain replied, "I fully understand how you must be feeling, because I feel the same, but try to see it from their point of view. To them, we have appeared out of nowhere in a far superior type of spacecraft, claiming to have come here from the future. You must admit that if you were in their shoes, you would be suspicious too. For all they know, we could be space terrorists, or even aliens in disguise, God forbid. Until we can get this sorted out, my advice to you is, be honest, stick to the facts, and don't give them cause for alarm".

Bill McLean raised his hand, wanting to speak again. "You've just said that we shouldn't give them cause for alarm. How can we, as ordinary passengers, give them cause for alarm?"

While indicating around the cabin with his hands, the captain replied. "We are all suspects here, and as such, we are to be interrogated separately. Now, as this questioning could possibly become difficult, we should try to remain calm and avoid getting angry in return. Having said that, I'll now tell you a bit more about what's going to happen next. You are to leave your personal belongings behind before you exit the spacecraft. This is to allow a team of technicians and security officials to come on board and carry out a thorough examination of everything we have here. We will be escorted to a holding area where the authorities will take over, and from then on, I'll no longer be in charge of you".

The passengers filed out of the spacecraft, followed closely by the crew. They were escorted down a concourse by armed guards to an aircraft hangar. Within several minutes, a high-ranking military officer appeared, followed by an oriental-looking woman dressed in a black jumpsuit. The woman stepped forward and called for attention. "Let me introduce myself. My name is Linda Wang. I am the nominated spokesperson for the world's council, and this here is General George Rufus, who is in charge of the military you can see here. Firstly, let me assure you that you will not come to any harm, provided you cooperate and follow our instructions without question. Our reasons for this are well justified, because you have just appeared out of nowhere in our part of the solar system, claiming to have come here from the future. I can tell you now that the council of nations have dismissed your claim as being totally false. Therefore, an arrest order has been placed on all of you until we can get to the truth of who you are and why you're here. As soon as it can be arranged, you will be questioned separately, but in the meantime, you will be kept in secure but comfortable solitary confinement".

Jim Ross raised a hand, requesting to speak. Looking in his direction, she gave a nod of consent, and Jim spoke. "As some of us are married couples, can we be accommodated together?" With a stern look on her face, she replied. "No, that will not be possible, as my instructions are to put you all into isolation for the time being. Now we will begin the screening process. If you turn and look behind you, you will see that there are desks with screen terminals. You are required to go and sit at one of those desks and follow the instructions you see on the screen in front of you. The first thing that will happen is that the computer will photograph you, then it will ask you the enter your identity details. Now go and choose your terminal, and when you have completed the process, raise your hand".

There was a faint sound of whimpering from a female passenger while this was going on, but Margaret Ross, who had managed to keep calm throughout, was the first to complete the questions and raised her hand. A guard appeared at her side, pinned a badge on her, then ordered her to follow him. Just before leaving the area, she turned and shouted to her husband. "Jim, try not to worry about me, because I'll be fine. Remember, I've been through worse than this, as well you know". Jim just nodded and gave her a wave before she went out of sight.

Margaret followed the guard to an accommodation block, where she was shown into a room with its door already open. He ushered her in, saying that she should find everything she needed in here, but if she did require anything else, there was an intercom on the bedside table that would link her to the administration. Laying a hand on his arm, Margaret asked. "How long am I likely to be held in here like this?" The guard removed her hand before replying. "I'm sorry Ma'am, but I'm unable to answer that question, but I can tell you that another guard will be coming for you in the morning to take you for questioning. I will be leaving now, so I'll bid you goodnight." With that, he left, closing and locking the door behind him.

Looking around the apartment, she was glad to see that it had a separate toilet with a shower and washbasin. On the bed was a freshly laundered nightdress with clean underwear. Next to that was a brand-new orange coloured jumpsuit, still in its wrapper. There was a note attached, which read. You are required to wear this suit at all times while in this facility. Fresh ones will be provided daily. On the bedside table next to the intercom was a food menu. She contacted the admin and ordered some coffee and sandwiches, then pre-ordered a light breakfast.

Ten minutes later, there was a knock at the door before it was opened by a female guard carrying a tray of sandwiches and coffee. She quietly laid them down on a small table by the window, then turned and left without saying a word. Once Margaret had finished her coffee and sandwiches, she went into the toilet to freshen up. She then undressed, put on the nightdress, and climbed into bed. It was good to be in a comfortable bed again after having spent such a long time being weightless, and it was not long before she fell asleep.

At 8 am, she was awakened by a knock at the door before it was opened and entered by the same female guard carrying her breakfast things. After laying them down, she lifted the old tray and spoke as she straightened up. "You must be ready by 9:30 sharp, as I will be coming to escort you for questioning". She did not say anything more and left, closing and locking the door again. By 9:15, Margaret was up and dressed in her jumpsuit, and at 9:30 precisely, the door was opened. The guard did not enter but beckoned her and said, "Follow me".

She was led along several passageways before being ushered into a small windowless room. The guard ordered her to sit at a table opposite a man and a woman, both dressed in green jumpsuits. The man was busy studying something on a monitor screen in front of him, and the woman just waited for the guard to take up a station at the door before speaking. "My name is Jill Cairns, and this here is my assistant Jack Cooper. Jack will be recording this interview and making notes of any key issues that may arise. The purpose of this investigation is for us to establish who you are, and why you're here. I must warn you though, as all your other crew members are being interviewed as I speak, and we can monitor those interviews from here, it would be unwise for you to attempt to deceive us".

Margaret gave a curt reply. "I would like to make this clear to you. I was not a member of the crew as you seem to suggest. I was merely a passenger on a space cruise". Jill cairns smirked as she continued. "Until it is proven otherwise, you will be treated as a crew member from a hostile spacecraft. Now let's begin by you telling us in your own words why you were on board the spacecraft, and what was the purpose of your mission".

Margaret drew a breath, then started to recall how she had been diagnosed with terminal cancer. She explained that her husband had sold his business to be able to pay for their last once-in-a-lifetime space cruise together. She continued and spoke in detail about their visit to the space station and how they had been amazed at the sheer enormity of it. Jill Cairns interrupted her at this point. "You have just said that you have cancer. At what stage is your cancer at now?" Margaret felt a bit embarrassed, not by the nature of the question, but more so by the answer she was about to give. "I don't have cancer anymore since having travelled backwards through time".

Jill looked at her over the top of her glasses and responded while still smirking. "How very strange that you claim to have had terminal cancer, but now you don't have it. I find this part of your story hard to believe, so you will need to come up with some way of proving to me that you're telling the truth". Considering the question for a moment, Margaret answered. "My husband, Jim Ross, will be telling the same story at his interview, and as you have just said yourself, you can monitor that from here". Still smirking, Jill replied. "Yes, we can, and of course he will, because you will no doubt have been in collusion with him". Margaret could feel herself getting irritated by Jill's sarcasm but managed to keep cool as she replied. "I also have my personal hand-held body scanner, which was loaned to me by the hospital for the duration of my illness. This scanner can tell me at any time how my cancer is progressing. However, after having come back through time, it has since given me a reading that the cancer is no longer evident. It also stores a record of all my previous readings, and this should serve to prove that I'm telling the truth in this respect". Jill raised an eyebrow and commented with a sarcastic tone, "How very interesting that you are in possession of such a futuristic device. I would very much like to see this device for myself, so where is it at the moment?"

Still managing to keep her cool, Margaret answered, "I left it on board the spacecraft with my belongings as instructed to do so by Captain Morgan". There was a pause as Jill was looking at something on the monitor screen. "Ah yes, I can see that this was a necessary security precaution, but since they have now been checked and cleared, I can have them brought here. Where exactly was your workstation on the spacecraft?" Realising now that she was still being considered as a crew member, Margaret gave her answer with a hint of her own sarcasm. "We were allocated seats in the second row of the passenger cabin."

There was another pause as Jill seemed to be communicating with someone through the monitor. "Okay she said, I have just issued an instruction for the security staff to locate your belongings and bring them directly here. In the meantime, you should continue with your story". Margaret nodded and continued her account of what happened after her visit to the space station.

She told how the ship was propelled at a fantastic speed towards Mars, and how it took only six days for them to reach there. After going into orbit, they were invited to go on a flying tour of the surface in one of the spaceship's shuttlecrafts. This tour flew them over and into the two most famous features on the planet, namely the Valles Marineris and then the giant extinct volcano Olympic Mons. She recalled the incident while flying into the crater of the Olympic Mons, how the shuttle had developed a malfunction that caused them to make a forced landing on its base. She was about to give her recollection of their spacewalk and their subsequent rescue, when there was a knock at the door of the interview room. The guard turned around and opened it to allow a security official to enter with a space bag. He laid it on the table, then turned and left the room without saying a word. Jill asked, "Does this bag contain your personal belongings?" Margaret nodded while drawing the bag towards herself. She opened it, withdrew her hand-held scanner, and switched it on. She was able to bring up the record of all her readings with the dates showing. It was interesting to see that the last date recorded was the 28th of July, 2059, whereas all the other readings prior to that, including those going back to when her cancer was first diagnosed, showed as being during 2069. Jill Cairns appeared to be lost for words at this point and conferred quietly with her assistant while perusing something on his screen.

Finally, after a few minutes, she spoke. "Okay, it seems that your husband has recounted the exact same story as you have just told us. Therefore we can see no useful purpose in continuing with this interview. You will be taken back to your room for the time being." As Margaret started to rise, she asked. "How long am I going to be kept a prisoner, and when will I be able to see my husband?" Jill replied. "As it's obvious to us now that you are indeed a married couple, we will allow your husband to share your room with you. He will be brought to you as soon as it can be arranged. Unfortunately, I'm unable to say how long you will remain under arrest because that decision is out of my hands. You will have to be patient until all our investigations have been concluded".

Margaret was escorted back to her room and was joined by Jim thirty minutes later.

"What do you make of all that nonsense?" he asked on his arrival. She greeted him with a hug as she replied. "Well, it seems at least they're satisfied that we're not space terrorists or even aliens, for that matter. I reckon it must have been the evidence of the scanner's record that convinced them that I had been telling the truth after all".

"Thank God for that", replied Jim, "I suppose we'll just have to wait now until all the other interviews have been completed, before we can be released".

It was two days later though, before a male guard opened the door and beckoned them to follow him. He led them through a series of passageways to a conference room, where all of the other passengers and crew were assembled. He advised them to find seats for themselves.

Facing them on a raised platform was a long table with five persons seated. In the middle of the table sat Linda Wang, and to their surprise, they saw that Mike Morgan, the captain of the spacecraft, was seated to her immediate left. At seeing this, Jim looked at Margaret and raised an eyebrow. She responded by putting a finger to her lips, cautioning him not to speak.

Linda Wang stood and spoke. "Before I tell you what the purpose of this meeting is, let me introduce the people we have seated here. The reasons for them being here will become evident as we progress. On my far right is Doctor Alan Jones MD, and to my immediate right is Professor Robert Gordon. To my immediate left is, as you know, Captain Mike Morgan, and seated next to him on my far left is Mr. Hans Zimmerman PHD. We have called this meeting to tell you that as a result of our investigations, we have concluded that you are not an intentional threat to us".

There were sighs of relief and murmurs around the room, but Linda Wang raised her hand, indicating that she wished to continue speaking. "However, that does not alter the fact that it has become extremely difficult for us to come to terms with the reality that you have somehow come here from the future. Although I did say that we now believe you are not an intentional threat to us, it has transpired that you may still present a danger to us. For that reason, your arrival here has been kept a closely guarded secret from the outer world. During the last two days, we have secretly consulted with leading scientists from around the world for their opinions on this delicate matter. I must tell you now that they have concluded that it would be unwise for us to allow you to go free into the outside world".

There were loud groans and voices from the four corners of the room, but Linda Wang just waited patiently until there was silence again before proceeding. "We have invited two of those eminent scientists to attend here and explain their reasons for their findings. Professor Robert Gordon, who has been studying for several years what the effects of time travel might be, will be the first to speak to you".

The professor got to his feet and spoke. "Good morning. I'm sure you must be wondering how you could possibly be a danger to us, therefore allow me to explain. The simple fact of the matter is that you should not be here because you belong to 2069. Now the problem we have with you being here at this time is that each one of you is already here as another self. Meaning, that there are now two of every one of you. How do we know this to be true, you may well ask. We know this to be true because we have secretly traced your origins, and sure enough, you're right there, doing whatever it was you were doing ten years ago".

There was a stunned silence within the room as the professor continued speaking. "Now, the danger of letting you go free is because you might try to get in touch with your families, and while that is understandable, we don't know for sure what would happen in the event of you ever meeting up with yourselves. There are sound theories from the scientists as well as some religious leaders that if you were ever to meet up with yourselves, you could inadvertently change the course of history. This, in turn, could trigger off a series of events that could have devastating consequences for the future and safety of the world. Having explained to you what the dangers are, you will be anxious to ask, what is to become of us. We have discussed this at length and have come up with two options for you to consider. The first option is that we provide homes for you at a top-secret location, where you will be able to live out your lives in relative luxury".

There were loud voices all around the room at this astonishing proposal, and a few hands shot up to request questions. The professor raised his hand to call for order before speaking again. "Please allow me to continue before asking questions. You will be given an opportunity to ask questions once I've explained what the second option is. The second option is that we attempt to send you back to your own time, but as the technicalities of achieving this, are well out of my sphere, I will ask my colleague Mr. Zimmerman to explain how this may be possible".

Hans Zimmerman got to his feet and spoke. "Good morning, I'm Hans Zimmerman, and I am a research scientist employed by the world's space agency to develop new types of rocket engines. Having had an opportunity of inspecting your magnificent spacecraft, I must admit that I was greatly impressed. We have been researching the feasibility of producing a nuclear-fueled rocket engine for some time now, and to discover that your spacecraft has a hybrid engine that can convert from conventional to nuclear fuel is amazing technology for us to see. I have been conferring with your captain Mike Morgan, and he told me that the reason you travelled through time was due to a fault in the engine's atomic governor. It seems that the governor was slow to kick in immediately after blasting away from Mars. He estimated that the ship had been travelling at the speed of light for about ten seconds before the governor took control again. With the benefit of this knowledge, I believe that if we were able to induce a controlled delay in the governor, we could make the spacecraft travel at the speed of light again. Now since you were coming from Mars when you went back through time, it's feasible to believe, that if you were going in the opposite direction and towards Mars, we might be able to achieve the opposite effect. Meaning that you should go forward in time. I have discussed this with my scientific colleagues, and although they have agreed it's possible, they have expressed reservations, stating that as it is only a theory, its success cannot be guaranteed. If, however, you were to ask for my own personal opinion, I truly believe the odds are much better than that, and as such, you should have nothing to lose by attempting to do it. Especially if the first option doesn't appeal to you". Hans Zimmerman finished by thanking everyone for their attention and sat down. Linda Wang then said. "I'm sure there are questions you are all itching to ask, so we'll take those now". Hands shot up all around the room, and Linda accepted the first question from the nearest person, which was Bill Mclean.

Bill got to his feet and spoke. "Both me and my wife come from working-class backgrounds, and we were only able to come on this cruise because we were lucky enough to win it in a major prize draw. If we were to choose the second option of returning to our own time, we would be choosing to go back to our ordinary hardworking lives again. Whereas the idea of us being able to live in relative luxury for the rest of our lives might appeal to us. I would therefore like to ask the professor for a bit more detail of what we could expect if we were to choose that option".

The professor remained seated while replying. "We have not finalized all the details yet but are looking at an uninhabited sub-tropical island in the Pacific Ocean. This island would be landscaped and developed to make it a really special place for you to live. You will be provided with good-quality homes and have everything you need for your well-being, comfort and pleasure. I have to make it clear, however, that although you will be free to go anywhere you like on the island, you will never be allowed to leave it. Nor will you ever be allowed to communicate with anyone in the outer world. If any of you do decide to give this option serious consideration, there will be ample time to discuss it further, before the spacecraft is ready to launch again".

Linda Wang selected the next person with their hand raised. It was Margaret Ross who stood and spoke. "As I explained at my interview, the reason for us being on the cruise was because of my incurable illness, but since having come back through time, my illness has disappeared. My question is this. If we were to choose the second option of returning to our own time, is there a danger my illness could return?" Linda Wang responded. "Since we have been expecting questions of a medical nature, we have invited Dr Jones along to deal with them.

Dr Jones stood and spoke. "Good morning Margaret. I've been looking at the transcript of your interview and fully understand your concerns. I think it would be inappropriate for us to openly discuss the type of preventive treatment we could offer you, so I will invite you to a private consultation as soon as this meeting is over". She thanked him and sat down.

Linda Wang then asked. "Are there any other medical questions?" As there was no response, the Doctor resumed his seat. Linda Wang took the next question from another passenger. He stood up and introduced himself. "My name is Omar Salem, and unlike the gentleman who spoke earlier, I come from a wealthy Kuwaiti family. As there's nothing to be gained for me choosing a life of luxury on a tropical island, I would much prefer to go home to my family. Can I ask Captain Morgan what he thinks our chances are for a successful outcome with the second option?"

Mike Morgan stood and replied. "As captain of the spacecraft, I'm confident that the ship is more than capable of taking us back into orbit and safely executing the manoeuvre suggested by Mr. Zimmerman. Whether or not we will successfully return to 2069 is as much an unknown to me as it will be for you. I will say this to you though, me and my crew are willing to give it our best shot. If, on the other hand, we fail to go forward in time, we will just have to return here and settle down to a life of luxury on a tropical island". The passengers laughed while giving him a round of applause. As there were no further questions, Linda Wang proceeded to wind up the meeting by saying that they were now free to go anywhere they liked within the complex. She also invited them to make full use of the leisure and recreational facilities that are available to them for the duration of their stay.

With the meeting closed, Margaret took hold of Jim's hand and pulled him towards Dr Jones. On seeing them approach, the doctor beckoned and guided them into an anti-room that had been set aside as a surgery. "Please be seated", he said. "Now Margaret, you must tell me all about the type of cancer you have had and what treatments, if any, were you given to suppress it." She shared her details from the time the first symptoms appeared, to the conclusion that it was terminal. When she finished, the doctor summarised. "I'm familiar with this rare form of cancer, and as you know, there is no known cure for it". Jim interrupted by saying, "Other than being able to come back through time I suppose". The doctor smiled as he responded. "Yes, that might be true, but there is no way of knowing for sure that it won't return in the future."

Margaret then spoke up. "You did mention at the meeting that you may be able to offer me some kind of preventive treatment." The doctor replied. "Yes, that's true, because since we have prior knowledge that you will get this particular type of cancer in the future, we should be able to identify and isolate the gene that caused it. Obviously, it would require you to have a small operation though." Margaret asked. "When would I be able to have this operation, and how successful will it be?" The doctor replied. "It has been proven to have had a high success rate. However, in preventive medicine, nothing can be completely guaranteed. You have to understand that most of the patients who have received this treatment were not guaranteed to get cancer anyway. We can only be guided by the statistics that all of the people who received the treatment did not get cancer in later years. We have an excellent hospital here within the complex that can perform this simple procedure, and I'm sure I could manage to arrange it for tomorrow, if that's suitable". Jim and Margaret both agreed that the time scale was suitable and thanked the doctor before leaving.

Margaret was operated on the very next day, and while in recovery, Dr Jones arrived to pay her a visit. "How are you feeling after the operation Margaret?" She smiled while replying, "I'm feeling fine, thank you doctor. When will I be allowed to leave the hospital?"

The doctor replied. "After rounds, I would imagine. Now, there is something I feel I should have pointed out to you before you agreed to have the treatment. You asked at the meeting if your cancer would return if you were to go forward in time again. I can assure you that under normal circumstances, your cancer will not return. However, travelling forward in time artificially is not a normal circumstance, and therefore I'm unable to give you a cast-iron guarantee that your cancer won't return if you were to choose that option. The way I see it is this. If your spacecraft does successfully go forward in time to 2069, will your body recognise that you had this operation back in 2059? Do you understand my meaning, Margaret?" She slowly nodded while replying. "Yes, I do understand where you are coming from with this, and I appreciate your honesty. This is now going to be a bit of a dilemma for us; however, we should have plenty of time to discuss it properly before the spacecraft is ready to launch again." The doctor smiled as he spoke. "I have to admire your sensible approach to your dilemma, but I don't envy you in your quest to make the right choice. I really wish you all the very best for the future, wherever that will be. I must leave you now, but if there are any other questions you can think of later, please don't hesitate to call on me at the surgery".

Jim collected Margaret from the hospital later in the afternoon, and as they were leaving, he asked, "Do you want to go straight back to the room, or is there something else you'd rather do?" She replied. "I don't want to go back to the room just yet, because all this confinement is making me stir crazy. I would much rather we go and find somewhere nice so that we can sit, relax, and discuss our options".

Jim replied, "Well, I know just the place, because I scouted the complex while you were in the hospital and found this cosy little coffee bar in one of the public areas". Margaret replied, "That sounds ideal to me, so lead the way sir".

They found a comfortable, secluded corner in the bar, and after fetching their coffees, Jim took her hand in his and asked. "Do you want to start with the discussion, or would you like me to begin?" She replied, "No, I'll begin by revealing my deepest thoughts, then you can carry on from there. If we were to choose to go home, there's a chance that my cancer would return, and if that were to happen, I'd only have a short time left to live. Whereas, if we choose to stay, then we should be guaranteed to have a long life together. Having said that, it would be easy for me to say, let's just agree to stay, but then again, I don't relish the thought of us not being able to see our loved ones again".

Jim gave her hand a squeeze and said, "Yes, I must admit that the thought of us not ever being able to see our families again would be hard to live with, but on the other hand, if we were to decide to go home and your cancer were to return, then that would be even harder for me to live with. Now, I've been doing a bit of thinking of my own, so here's what I think. Our other selves, who rightfully belong here at this time, are already living with our families, and if we decide to stay, then we'll have to accept that we won't ever be allowed to see them, however, try looking at it another way. We'll always be able to content ourselves with the satisfaction of knowing that they're all safe and well. Your other self, meaning Margaret from 2059, is unaware of our existence, and she doesn't know either that she is going to get cancer. If we decide to stay, then I suggest we have a word with Dr Jones to ask him if it would be possible for her to have the same preventive treatment as you have had. Just think, we would be assuming the role of her guardian angels by giving her the gift of a full life. What's more, Jim won't have to sell up his business for them to go on a space cruise in ten years' time".

Margaret laughed as she replied. "You know, I like the sound of your logic and agree we should talk to the doctor about it. Let's go and visit him first thing in the morning".

Just then, Bill and Sandra McLean entered the bar and, on seeing them both seated, asked if they could join them. "Yes, of course you can," Margaret replied, "it'll give us an opportunity to hear your views on both the options". Sandra started by saying, "Bill and I have decided to stay, because we have nothing to go back to. We never had children, and both our parents have passed on. The professor has shown us three-dimensional computer-generated images of what the island is going to look like when it's finished. I can tell you; we were greatly impressed because it looks like it's going to be a tropical paradise".

Margaret turned to Jim and asked. "Do you think we should go and see the images for ourselves, dear?"

"Yes, definitely," he replied, "so where are they being shown?" It was Sandra who answered. "There's an audio-visual display set up in the conference room, and the professor will be in attendance in the forenoons to answer any questions."

"That's ideal," said Margaret, "because we're planning to pay a visit to Dr Jones in the morning, and his surgery happens to be in the same area". They ordered more coffees and spent the remainder of the afternoon chatting and reminiscing about their space adventures together.

The following morning Jim a Margaret ventured out to visit Dr Jones in his surgery. The doctor welcomed them in by asking, "How can I help you this morning Margaret?"

She answered by telling him about their discussion, and how they had decided to ask him if it would be possible for her other self, meaning Margaret from 2059, to have the same preventive treatment as she has had. She continued by explaining their reasons for this request, then waited for his response.

The Doctor raised an eyebrow and replied, "I must admire your unselfish motives for wanting to do this and wonder why on earth I never thought of it myself. I think this is a splendid idea, and we should seriously look at how to go about making it happen. Who was your GP back in 2059?" Margaret thought for a moment and then said, "It was Doctor Brown from our local medical centre". She managed to recall the telephone and address details and gave them to the doctor. With the benefit of this information, he started a search on his computer, and after a few minutes, he said, "Okay, I've managed to trace him, but as this is a sensitive issue, you'll have to leave it with me for the time being. I'll get back to you as soon as I have any news for you". They both thanked him and left his surgery to enter the conference room.

Some of the other passengers and crew were already seated, waiting for a re-run of the audio-visual display, and Margaret and Jim found seats for themselves at the back. The display started with what looked like a package holiday advert. It showed swaying palms on the edge of a stunning shoreline, with waves from the bluest sea ever lapping onto a golden sandy beach. It continued in three dimensions with a voice-over describing and illustrating the kind of homes that were being planned for them. These intended homes were to be of a mini colonial style with swimming pools and manicured gardens. The computer produced virtual images of the living spaces with the most up-to-date furnishings and fittings, including home entertainment devices. In the next scene, two actors were seen sitting on the front porch enjoying cocktails, while another showed the leisure activities they could expect to enjoy. There was to be golf, tennis, fishing, and a range of other water sports. For their evening's entertainment, it was planned to have a community hub, beach bars, and restaurants. The display ran on for about twenty minutes, with the voice-over doing an excellent job of convincing them of a promised life of luxury.

Just before it ended, they decided to go in search of the professor.

He was using another anti room as his office, and they gave a light knock on his door, which was promptly opened by the professor himself. He invited them to enter by saying, "Do come in. I assume you're here because you have some questions for me".

Jim replied, "Yes, we do have one or two".

"Excellent", said the professor. "Then you can fire away, and I'll do my best to answer them".

Jim started by asking. "How many of the passengers have shown an interest in staying?"

The professor replied. "Although there has been a lot of interest shown, there's not many that have chosen to stay yet. I have two positives with six other couples still thinking about it".

Jim responded by saying, "This is what we can't quite grasp because, according to the audio-visual display, there's going to be a whole range of activities on offer. How are you going to manage to do all of that for such a small number of people?"

The professor replied by saying, "We have envisaged that there might not be many of you staying, and that's another reason for the admin staff to live on the island along with you. These volunteer workers will have their families with them and will be housed in the same standard of homes as yourselves.

"During their free time, they will also be allowed access to the same recreational facilities. There is something else we have had to consider, and that is the fact that the spacecraft may well fail to go forward in time. If that were to happen, every one of the passengers and crew will have no other choice but to return here and settle down to a life on the island. On the other hand, if they do successfully go forward in time, then we would plan to set up a top-secret research facility on a part of the island to study the effects of time travel. Now because you will be able to interact socially with the research and admin staff, you will be required to sign a contract agreeing to keep it secret from them the real reasons for your being there. They will be told that you are part of a protection program and have been sent to live on the island for security purposes, and that's all they will need to know. A word of caution, though. If you were to break the agreement, then we would have no alternative but to incarcerate you for the remainder of your lives. That's the worst scenario though, and I sincerely hope that it never comes to that. Now I've been as honest as I can in answering those questions. Do you have anything else you would like to ask?"

Margaret responded, "Yes, I have a question. What is the time scale for all of this to be put into place?" The professor replied, "We are looking at three months before your new homes will be ready for occupation, then in stages of up to a year for everything else to be completed. In the meantime, we intend to build temporary accommodation for you on the island. The alternative to that is that you remain here until everything is ready?"

Margaret replied. "I think we would prefer to go and live in the temporary accommodation rather than having to stay here any longer than is necessary".

"Very good," said the professor. "Think it over, and let me know your decision before the spacecraft is ready to launch". They both thanked him before leaving his office.

Doctor Jones was waiting for them outside the professor's office. "I'm glad I've managed to catch you, because I've got a bit of news for you. Come into my surgery and I'll explain".

They followed him into his surgery and sat down. "Okay," he said, "here's how it is so far. I've contacted your Dr Brown and explained to him about your request. He agrees that your other Margaret should have the same treatment as soon as possible. He also completely understands the need for secrecy and has made a vow not to tell her anything about you. We have hatched a plan on how best to approach her with the scary news that she is going to get cancer in the future. He is going to tell her that this knowledge was picked up as a result of her having had a recent blood test, but she will also be told about the preventive treatment on offer. The doctor will explain that it's a relatively simple procedure and will strongly advise her to have it done sooner rather than later. All we will need then is her consent, and we can arrange to have the operation done within a few days. Now, if she agrees to have the operation and it goes ahead as planned, then this raises another question for you. This new development could influence your decision on whether you would prefer to stay in this time or return to the future. The way I see it is this. Since both of you will have had the preventive treatment, I can't see how the cancer can possibly return in this time or at any other time in the future. Do you see what I'm getting at here Margaret?"

"Yes, I do," Margaret replied, "but since she is really me after all, she will no doubt do the right thing and agree to have the operation. We had almost made up our minds to stay, but as you rightly point out, this could make us change our minds. However, we would prefer to wait until it has been confirmed that she has had the treatment before we make our final choice".

"Excellent," said the doctor, "I'll let you know as soon as I hear anything. Hopefully that should be in a couple of days". They both thanked him and left to go for some lunch. During lunch, they discussed this new development and decided that if they did hear that her other self has had the operation, then they should make up their minds to go home to the future.

After lunch, they decided to pay Mr. Zimmerman a visit to get an update on the spacecraft's progress and to find out when it was likely to be launched. He explained that the craft was now on the launch pad, where a series of essential maintenance safety checks were being carried out. He said that he was hopeful that these checks would be completed within a couple of days. Then it would be a case of getting everyone on board when the weather conditions were favourable. He advised them that if they were seriously thinking about going, then they should make themselves available for boarding within 24 hours after the checks had been completed.

Two days had passed, and as they had not heard anything from Dr Jones, they decided to pay him another visit. "Come in he said, I was just about to send for you. Unfortunately, Margaret number two hasn't had her operation yet, but the good news is that she has agreed to have it done. Dr Brown has worked the oracle with her local hospital, and as a result, she has been allocated a time to have it done first thing tomorrow".

"That's great news said Jim, but it's cutting it a bit fine because we're expecting to be told anytime soon to prepare ourselves for boarding."

"Oh, I see," said the Doctor, "then I assume you've made up your minds to go".

Margaret replied, "Yes, that was to be our intention if we knew for sure that the other Margaret had had the operation. However, we have to be absolutely certain that it has been done because things can go wrong, as you know. She might have a change of heart at the last minute and want to postpone it, or the hospital might find a reason to delay it. If these things were to happen, then there's no way we can risk boarding the spacecraft".

The doctor replied. "Yes, I understand why you would be worried about this, and I'll speak to Mr. Zimmerman about it. I'm sure another day won't make a difference to the launch schedule. In the meantime, let's keep our fingers crossed and hope that the operation goes ahead as planned". Feeling a bit disappointed, they said goodbye to the doctor, and left him to go back to their room.

The following morning, they were wakened by the intercom bleeping, and Jim stretched across to press the receiver button. The voice on the other end spoke. "Good morning, I hope I haven't called you too early, but I've been instructed to tell you that the preparations for the launching have begun, and you are required to attend a prep meeting in the conference room at 11 am".

At eleven o'clock, they entered the conference room along with all the other passengers and crew. Professor Gordon, Hans Zimmerman, and Captain Morgan were already seated at the table on the raised platform. The professor got to his feet and spoke. "Good morning, please find yourselves seats, and we'll begin". Once everyone was seated, the professor began. "Just for your information, there are only three couples who have opted to stay behind. These are Bill and Sandra McLean, Ian and Catlin Wells, and two of the cabin crew, George Douglas and Connie Elliot. I'm sure you would like to join me in wishing them all the very best of luck with their new lives". There was a round of applause before the professor continued. "There's not much left for me to say just now, other than to wish you all a safe launch and a successful journey back to the future. I'll now hand you over to Mr. Zimmerman, who will fill you in on the launch procedure".

Hans Zimmerman got to his feet and spoke. "We have fixed the time for the launching as being 12 noon tomorrow. At 9 am, you will assemble here for a short briefing before being taken by coach to the launch site. While at this facility, you will be decontaminated and helped into your space suits before ascending on an elevator to the access hatch of the spacecraft. Are there any questions?"

Margaret Ross raised her hand and asked, "Has Dr Jones spoken with you about our predicament?"

Hans Zimmerman replied, "Yes, he did speak to me, and while I understand and sympathise with your predicament, I'm unable to delay the launch any longer. It has been arranged beforehand to have all domestic aircraft diverted away from an area of a hundred square miles of the launch site. There is also to be a perfect weather window for a safe launch tomorrow, and if we were to delay it further, we would lose that window for another week or two. The doctor did also say that he was expecting to hear soon the news that you are anxiously waiting for. Therefore, may I suggest that you leave this meeting now and go and pay him a visit". The question-and-answer session continued as Jim and Margaret filed out.

Dr Jones was communicating with someone through his monitor as they entered the surgery, and he smiled while indicating with his hand for them to be seated. When he was finished, he shut down his monitor and looked up, smiling as he spoke. "That was Dr Brown I have just been conferring with. He has confirmed that your other Margaret has had the operation and is now in recovery. You don't know how glad I am to be able to give you this news and to wish you a safe trip back to your own time. When you do get home, I'll be ten years older, but I would very much like for you to look me up, if I happen to be still around, that is".

Margaret replied while smiling, "Yes of course, Doctor, it'll be our pleasure because we owe you a great debt of gratitude for all you've done for us, and I'm sure you will still be around in ten years' time. At that point, they shook hands with him before leaving to go back to their room.

On their way back, they bumped into Bill and Sandra, who were just heading out. Margaret told them the good news that she had been desperately waiting for, and how she had been reassured that it would now be safe for her to go forward in time. She commented that she had been surprised to have heard that Ian and Catlin Wells, the young honeymooners, had also chosen to remain. Sandra explained that Catlin had recently discovered that she was pregnant, and after a consultation with Dr Jones, they decided to stay as she did not want to risk losing the baby by attempting to go forward in time. They chatted for several more minutes, before saying their final farewells and going their separate ways.

At 9 am the following morning, the passengers and crew assembled in the conference room. Captain Morgan was there with the professor and Hans Zimmerman. The professor greeted them by saying, "Good morning, everyone. This is your big day, and you'll be glad to know that your spacecraft is primed and waiting for you. Now, as Captain Morgan has a few words of his own that he would like to say, I'll hand you over to him".

Mike Morgan spoke, "As the professor has rightly said, our spacecraft is ready to launch, but I should mention that for us to be able to travel at the speed of light, we need a blast from nuclear fission, but we're unable to have that blast, without nuclear fuel rods. Now as you know, our rods are on board the shuttlecraft, which was tethered to the space station. Assuming it's still there, we then have the problem of how we are going to get it back on board. Mr. Zimmerman has come up with a solution to our problem, though, by kindly lending us a robotic craft that has mechanical arms with hands attached. As this robotic craft can be operated remotely, we will guide it over to where the shuttlecraft is anchored to the station. Once there, we will locate the anchor, and with the assistance of the mechanical hands, we hope to be able to release it. If happily affected, the shuttlecraft will then be brought back to the spaceship, and the fuel rods can then be re-installed. As simple as that! I will add that the robot will also be brought back on board so that Mr. Zimmerman can have it back in ten years' time".

Everyone laughed, including Hans Zimmerman, at Mike's attempt at dry humour. Hans Zimmerman then added his own best wishes to everyone before they were escorted out and onto the coach for transfer to the launch site. At the launch site, they were decontaminated and assisted with their space suits before ascending to the entrance hatch of the spacecraft.

Once everyone was on board and securely strapped in, the entrance hatch was closed and sealed. Mike Morgan's voice then came over the broadcast. "Okay folks, here we go again. I'm just about to complete my prelaunch checks, so you had better prepare yourselves for lift-off in a few minutes from now".

The electronic voice announced, "Ten seconds to lift off. 10, 9, 8, 7, 6, 5, 4, 3, 2, 1, CONTACT".

Part 3

The rocket engine roared into life, lifting the spacecraft effortlessly off the launch pad. It took about five minutes to break free from the earth's gravitational pull and for the sensation of weightlessness to kick in again. Mike Morgan's voice came over the broadcast. "I'm sure you will agree with me when I say that this has been as smooth a launch as you're ever likely to have. We will be orbiting the earth to get us into the correct trajectory for a rendezvous with the space station, so you will have another opportunity to enjoy the views".

After twice around the world, the space station came into view, and to everyone's relief, they could see that the shuttlecraft was still securely tethered to it. The captain edged the ship as close as possible to the station as his voice came through. "We are about to launch the robot to head off and hopefully release the shuttlecraft". The passengers heard the bomb bay doors opening and watched through their observation ports as a small comical looking craft with mechanical arms on its front sped away towards the station.

The crewman, who was remotely piloting the robot, located the tether cable on his monitor screen and guided it along its length until he could see where the device was anchored. He carefully manipulated the mechanical hands to begin the task of releasing it, and after a few minutes, the shuttle came free. Mike Morgan spoke again. "You'll be glad to know folks, that it's so far so good, because we have managed to free the shuttle and are about to bring her back on board along with our little hero, the robot. When that is done, we will begin reinstalling the nuclear fuel rods, but as this work can take up to three hours, you will have to be patient for a while longer before we can be on our way".

It was exactly three hours before they heard Mike speak again. "Okay folks, the rods have been installed, and we're now ready to blast back to the future. As I said before, although we are weightless, the initial surge may cause you to float around a bit. Therefore, make sure that your seat restraints are securely fastened because here we go!"

"STANDBY FOR BLAST OFF", announced the electronic voice. "10, 9, 8, 7, 6, 5, 4, 3, 2, 1, CONTACT".

There was the familiar sound of the muffled explosion from the rear of the craft, and the cabin immediately filled up with a blinding flash of light. This light lasted for about ten seconds before returning to normal. They were now travelling at an incredible speed as the captain spoke. "Well folks, it seems, at least, we have managed to achieve having the flash of light, but whether or not we have succeeded in moving forward in time, remains to be confirmed. In the meantime, I'll have to concentrate on stopping this ship before we go too far. Once that's done, I'll attempt to contact the new international space station.

The passengers could see that the speed of the ship was being reduced, albeit slowly.

Margaret Ross's heart was thumping as she switched on her hand-held body scanner. It was painfully slow to boot up and indicated that scanning was in progress. Finally, it settled, and to her great relief, it stated that there was no trace of cancer. It also recorded the date as being the 28th of July, 2070. "Look Jim," she cried, "look at my scanner, for it is showing the date as being 2070, which is exactly one year after we were preparing to leave Mars. It's also telling me that there is no trace of cancer".

He looked across and spoke, "Yes, so I see, and what a great relief it is to know that you're finally free from that terrible disease, and if that date is correct, then we have actually moved forward in time by eleven years".

It was about an hour before the ship came to a stop, and the captain made an announcement. "As you can see, we've managed to stop the ship, but not before we have travelled a third of the way to Mars. We will now prepare for our return journey, but before we do that, our engineers will be making some essential adjustments to the atomic governor, because we don't want to risk taking another trip through time. While this work is in progress, I'll try to contact the space station. I'll leave the ship's broadcast turned on, so that you can all listen in to the transmissions. The passengers listened quietly as the captain spoke on the radio.

"This is Captain Morgan calling the international space station."

There was no response, only a squishing and squealing radio noise.

The captain tried again. "This is Captain Morgan calling the international space station."

After a period of silence, there came a reply. "This is the international space station. Identify your craft."

There were cheers from the passengers at hearing this response, and the captain replied, "We are the Galaxy spacecraft number 1, returning from our space cruise to Mars in 2069".

There was no immediate response from the space station this time until a different voice came on.

"This is Commander Hall speaking. I am responsible for the space station's security. We have no record of any space cruise leaving here in 2069. Therefore, you had better come up with a valid explanation of who you are."

The captain responded by recounting the whole story from beginning to end about their space cruise to Mars and how they had accidentally travelled backwards through time. He spoke about their time on Earth when they were held in custody until they had managed to prove their innocence. He mentioned the two scientists, Professor Robert Gordon and Mr. Hans Zimmerman, who were instrumental in helping them get back to their own time.

There was a brief pause before the commander spoke again.

"Okay, I've listened to your fantastic tale, and quite frankly, I find it impossible to believe. However, after careful consideration, I've decided to allow you the benefit of the doubt for the time it takes for me to confer with my superiors. In the meantime, you are warned not to approach the space station. In other words, stay exactly where you are until I make contact with you again".

There was a stunned silence within the passenger cabin as everyone was trying to come to terms with what they had just heard, until Mike Morgan's voice came over the broadcast. "You will all have heard the commander's comments and will be just as confused as me as to why there's no record of us leaving the space station in 2069. Let's hope that it's just an administrative error which will be sorted out in due course".

It was several hours before the commander's voice was heard again.

"I apologise for the delay Galaxy 1, but I had to confer with my superiors for advice and confirmation that you are who you say you are. It seems that we have been expecting you for over a year now, and as such, I've been instructed to tell you that you are now allowed to approach the space station. When you do arrive back here, however, you will be met and de-briefed by representatives of the council of nations before you will be allowed to return to Earth".

The engine fired up, propelling the ship at its now controlled speed of 400 thousand miles an hour, but since they had gone a third of the way to Mars, it would take a further two days for their return journey.

During the afternoon of the second day, the passengers were relieved to see the new international space station through their personal observation ports. The ship edged slowly closer, until it locked into one of the docking ports. "Here we are at last," announced Mike Morgan. I'm sure you must all be as relieved as me to know that our space odyssey is nearly over". The passengers gave a round of applause and waited for their further instructions.

About 10 minutes later, Mike's voice came on again. "I have just this minute received our instructions. We are to exit the spacecraft, taking all of our personal belongings with us; the reason for this will be explained later. I should add that transports have been provided to take us to meet the representatives".

The passengers and crew left the spacecraft and boarded the electric vehicles. They moved off in convoy and travelled along the brightly lit bending tunnel for several minutes, until they came to a side opening with a pedestrian walkway leading off. The driver advised them to follow the walkway to the end, where they would be met by a hostess at the entrance to a meeting room.

They filed into the room and were pleasantly surprised to see that fresh coffee had been provided for them. The room was set out with tables and chairs arranged in a semi-circle, facing a top table. The hostess invited them to help themselves to the refreshments, adding that she was expecting the representatives to arrive shortly. Everyone took advantage of the refreshments, before taking them to their preferred seating positions. Jim and Margaret chose two seats closest to the top table and sat sipping their coffees while waiting for the representatives to arrive. Margaret turned to Jim and asked, "What do you make of the fact that we had to remove our personal possessions from the spacecraft?"

"I'm not sure," he replied, "but I get the feeling that something is not right".

Margaret commented, "Yes, I agree, for something is telling me that we won't be going home anytime soon". There were whispered conversations going on around the room, until two men entered, making their way quickly to the top table. As they turned to face them, everyone was gobsmacked to see that the two representatives were none other than Professor Robert Gordon and Mr. Hans Zimmerman.

The professor smiled as he spoke, "I bet you didn't expect to be seeing us here on the space station after all these years. We only just arrived from Earth this morning on a space shuttle, and I'm happy to report that although we have aged somewhat, we are still in good shape. Firstly, I must apologise to you on behalf of the council for this delay and for the predicament you are about to find yourselves in, therefore allow me to explain. After your lift-off, we tracked you all the way until you simply disappeared from the radar. We correctly concluded that you had successfully moved forward in time again, and although initially, we rejoiced at your success, there came the realisation that the world had now entered a new age of time travel. You will remember that I had mentioned back in 2059 that if you were successful in moving forward in time again, we would plan to set up a top-secret research facility on the island to study the effects of time travel. As a result of that research, it has been concluded that time travelling will be too dangerous for us. Therefore some changes were going to have to be made. I will now ask Mr. Zimmerman to continue from here, and explain to you what these changes were and how they will affect you".

With a solemn look on his face, Hans Zimmerman started to speak. "I find this very difficult because I suspect that you're not going to like what I'm about to tell you. As I mentioned at our first meeting back in 2059, I had been working on ways of trying to develop nuclear-powered rocket engines. When I found that your spacecraft had such a thing, it was a real bonus for me, because this new technology was there for me to develop further. Alas, it was not to be because the council considered otherwise, and they have pulled the plug on all future development projects, relating to nuclear-powered rocket engines. Thus, the reason why there was no space cruise leaving the space station in 2069. Furthermore, an international law has been passed, banning all future attempts to time travel, and as your spacecraft has the ability to travel through time, it is now considered to be an illegal craft. The result being that it will not be allowed to return to earth".

There were gasps and murmurs from around the room at hearing this news, until Mike Morgan sprang to his feet and asked. "What's going to happen to my spacecraft if it's not going to be allowed to return to earth?"

Hans Zimmerman drew a breath and said, "My orders were to have it destroyed". Mike was about to protest, but Hans raised his hand, stopping him. "Please allow me to continue, because although I did say that my orders were to have it destroyed, I have managed to persuade them otherwise, on the grounds that it would be a sacrilege to destroy such a magnificent piece of technology. Although my reasons have been accepted, they are still not going to allow it to return to earth. This then presented them with the problem of what they should do with it. A think tank of leading scientists was assembled, and several ideas were considered, until they settled on what was to be their favoured option. The plan now is to convert the spacecraft into a giant time capsule, and propel it into deep interstellar space, never to return".

Mike Morgan bristled and shouted. "Like hell you will! That spacecraft is the sole property of Galaxy Space Cruises Ltd, and as I am her legal captain, I point blank refuse to allow you to take over my ship". Hans Zimmerman stood silent with a stony expression, until Professor Gordon interrupted, saying, "I'm sorry to have to inform you, Captain Morgan, but there is no such organisation as Galaxy Space Cruises Ltd, because they were never established. Furthermore, as these orders come from the highest authority in the world, you will have no other choice but to comply with them."

Looking somewhat beaten, Mike Morgan sat down. Hans Zimmerman resumed speaking. "I fully understand how you must be feeling about this Mike, but do try to look at it another way. Wouldn't it be a fitting end for such a magnificent spacecraft to spend her days wandering among the stars forever. Who knows where she might end up". With almost a tear in his eye, Mike just nodded. Hands shot up around the room, and Hans Zimmerman took the first question from the nearest person, who happened to be Jim Ross.

Jim asked, "What's going to happen to us, if there is no spacecraft to take us home?"

Hans answered. "You will be ferried back to earth on one of the space shuttles, but once there, you will be immediately transported to the island. Which, I might add, is now like a tropical paradise".

Jim asked. "Why are we being sent to the island when we have successfully come back to our own time? Surely, we can't change the course of history now".

The professor indicated to Hans Zimmerman that he would like to answer this question. "Yes, that's perfectly true, but you may still be a danger to yourselves, or indeed your other selves, who are still there, since there was no space cruise in 2069. Although we do believe that the world is relatively safe from you, we still don't know for sure what would happen in the event of you ever meeting up with yourselves. You see, in reality, you don't exist in today's world, and we are of an opinion that if you were ever to meet up with your other selves, the laws of physics might dictate that one of you should simply disappear".

There was a look of shock and horror on everyone's face and a period of silence fell about the room, until Omar Salem got onto his feet and said, "Whilst I can understand that meeting up with our other selves might be dangerous for us or for them, what about the rest of our families. Would we, for instance, be able to meet up with them whilst avoiding a direct contact with our immediate other selves?"

The professor replied, "In theory, that might be possible, but try putting yourself into their shoes. Imagine how you would react if someone turned up on your doorstep, claiming to be your close relative with a fantastic tail that they are a time traveller. I think you would be calling the police. However, this is something we will continue to look at, but for the time being, you will have no option but to go and settle on the island". Omar thanked the professor for his honesty and sat down.

The next question came from one of the other passengers. "When can we expect to be taken back to Earth?"

The professor answered by saying, "We have enough room for all of you on board the same shuttle craft as we arrived on this morning, but as it still has a fair bit of business to conduct with the space station, I imagine that it will be a few days before it's ready to depart. In the meantime, we can accommodate you in our very comfortable space hotel.

At that point, Mike Morgan got onto his feet again and asked, "Since we're all being transported back to Earth in a few days, when were you planning to send my ship off into interstellar space?"

"As soon as it can be arranged," replied Hans Zimmerman, "but that depends on whether or not you will cooperate with us in making this happen. Failing that, we will have to rely on our own technicians to go on board and work out how to do this by themselves. That, as you know, could take some time to accomplish, and in that event, it's unlikely you will still be here to see it happen. If, on the other hand, they fail to make it work, then we will have no other choice but to revert to our original option of having her destroyed".

Mike replied, "Well, in that case, you give me no choice but to cooperate with you because I don't want my ship destroyed. I did say that I'm not prepared to give her up. Therefore, it's only right and proper that it should be me as her captain to be the one that propels her away on her final voyage".

Hans Zimmerman replied, "Yes of course Mike, and I totally agree with you. I'm also glad that you have decided to accept the inevitable, because there really is no alternative. Having said that, when and how would you propose to do it?"

Mike considered the question for a moment before replying. "I think we could do it sometime tomorrow at the earliest, if that's agreeable. I would plan to go on board in the afternoon with my crew to begin the starting routines. Once they are complete, I will undock the ship and manoeuvre her into a position and direction of your choice, before setting a delay timer for the countdown to commence. This delay will give us enough time to leave the ship on the shuttlecraft and return to the space station before she blasts away. Oh, and before I forget, would you like me to bring back your robot?"

Hans laughed as he replied, "That's very thoughtful of you Mike, but as it's now obsolete, we'll just leave it as an addition to the time capsule".

The professor then added, "Since we're all in agreement, that should conclude the main purpose of this meeting, but I do have something else I need to tell you before we wind it up. As was mentioned earlier, the plan is to convert the spacecraft into a giant time capsule before sending her off on her never to return voyage. We have brought with us from earth, another capsule that contains personal messages and objects from each of the world's leaders. I've also been instructed to invite all of you to contribute to this capsule by adding your own personal messages along with any objects you might like to donate. The leaders wanted to make this offer to you as a gesture of goodwill, as it would be a fitting tribute to yourselves for being the only humans to have ever travelled through time. Please think it over, and if you do decide that you would like to be a contributor, you can do this tomorrow before the capsule is taken on board. Finally, we have an excellent viewing gallery here on the space station, and you're all invited to come and witness the historic event for yourselves. I suggest that we meet up in this gallery immediately after lunch tomorrow, when you can put your items into the time capsule before it is closed up. Captain Morgan and his team will then depart with it to prepare the ship for launch. Now, as your transports are waiting to take you to your hotel, you can enjoy the rest of your day and evening, and we'll see you all tomorrow. I should mention that the same transports will pick you up shortly after lunch tomorrow and bring you directly to the gallery.

The following day after lunch, the passengers and crew members were assembled in the hotel's foyer, waiting for the transports to arrive. Mike Morgan and six of his crewmen were already kitted up in their space suits in preparation for boarding the spaceship. Margaret Ross had spent the previous night writing up her account of their space adventure and how the effects of time travel had served to rid her of cancer. She intended to put this into the time capsule along with the personal body scanner.

Within a few minutes, the transports arrived, and everyone filed out of the hotel and boarded them. The vehicles moved off together, travelling in a clockwise direction along the tunnel for several minutes, until they came to a junction with another tunnel leading off to the right. They turned into this tunnel, and the driver explained that they were now travelling along one of the main spokes of the space station, heading towards the central hub.

They pulled up in front of an entrance, and the driver told them that they would find elevators inside that will take them directly to the gallery.

Sure enough, within the entrance, there was a hallway with four glass elevators waiting with their doors open. Margaret and Jim chose the nearest one, and when it reached its maximum number of people allowed, the door closed automatically. It rose rapidly, making only one stop, which happened to be the viewing gallery. They stepped out into a star gazer's dream, for it was like a huge planetarium. It had a clear roof giving a 360-degree all-round view of the heavens. There was a passageway going around the perimeter of a circular raised seating area, looking down on a round lecture platform. A cigar-shaped tube was sitting in the middle of the platform between two support trestles, and standing over it, were the professor and Hans Zimmerman.

The professor spoke, "Good afternoon. Please find yourselves seats, and we will explain what is going to happen. Firstly, what you see here is the capsule we have brought with us from Earth. When we have finished adding your own contributions, we will close it up so that Captain Morgan and his team can take it with them when they leave to board the spacecraft. On completion of his routines, he will undock the craft and bring her 'round to a position directly above us so that we will all have an unrestricted view of it. You will be able to recline your seats and lie back in comfort to watch the blast off as it happens. Now for those of you who wish to add your personal contributions, you should come down here in an orderly fashion. The reason being that we will have to inspect each item before inserting it for security purposes. A short queue was formed leading down through an aisle in the seated area. It was noticeable, however, that neither Mike Morgan nor any of his team were attempting to join the queue. Each item was thoroughly inspected by Hans

Zimmerman before placing it into the capsule, and he had a puzzled look on his face as he turned Margaret's body scanner over in his hands. She explained what it was and her reasons for donating it. He nodded with a smile and carefully inserted it along with her story. When the last of the passenger's items had been put into the capsule, the professor looked up in the direction of Mike Morgan and said, "Captain Morgan, I've noticed that neither you nor any of your team have made an attempt come down. Are you quite sure you don't want to add anything of your own to this capsule?"

Mike nodded and replied, "Yes, we're quite sure, thank you".

With a wry smile, the professor said, "As you wish, it's entirely your choice".

After closing the capsule, he straightened and made a short speech. "We are sending this capsule off into interstellar space in the hope that sometime in the future, it might be found and appreciated by some intelligent life form from a far-off galaxy. Now Captain Morgan, if you would please send two of your team down here to fetch this capsule, you can be on your way to start your routines".

The captain nodded and delegated two of his crew to go down for it. The two crewmen collected the capsule and returned with it to join Mike and the rest of his team. Hans Zimmerman then spoke. "Mike, you did say that you will manoeuvre the craft into a direction of our choosing, but as you have the greater knowledge, we have decided to leave that choice to you. Obviously though, it should be in the opposite direction to the sun. We will be able to communicate directly with you so that you can keep us informed of your progress. Mike Morgan then came to attention and saluted before turning away to go onto the elevators, followed by his crew.

Hans Zimmerman then spoke. "As we will have a bit of a wait until the captain has completed his routines, I'll explain how we are going to communicate with him. A radio contact will be established via the station's control room. This contact will be relayed to us so that we can all hear him talking through the speakers around the gallery. He lifted a device, and while holding it high for all to see, he said, "Likewise, he will be able to hear my voice when I speak into this. As I assume he will be busy doing whatever it is he has to do before he can get started, I'll let him get on with it undisturbed. In the meantime, please feel free to wander around the outer edge of the gallery, as the views of the rest of the station from here are quite amazing.

It was just under an hour before Mike's voice was heard in the gallery. "This is Captain Morgan calling Hans Zimmerman. Are you receiving me?"

Speaking into his handset, Hans replied, "Yes Mike, we can hear you perfectly. How are things going at the moment?"

"Everything is fine," Mike replied, "we're just about to undock and bring the craft 'round to a position directly above you. You had better be ready for us coming, because this will only take about five minutes."

Everyone rushed to get into their reclined seats in preparation for seeing the ship appear above them. Within a few minutes, the giant spacecraft slowly came into view. The passengers and remaining crew members gave a hearty cheer and applauded loudly as she came to a stop directly overhead.

Mike's voice came through the speakers, "I'm now going to turn the craft so that she is pointing in my chosen direction before we depart".

As the spacecraft was slowly turning, the professor spoke, "We should shortly be seeing the shuttle craft leaving the mother ship to bring Captain Morgan and his crew back to the station. Everyone was laid back in their seats, patiently waiting for the shuttlecraft to appear, but after thirty minutes, when there was no sign of it, Hans Zimmerman lifted his handset and spoke into it, "Captain Morgan, this is Hans Zimmerman speaking. Have you got a problem with trying to launch the shuttlecraft?"

There was a moment of silence until there came a reply. "Yes, I do have a bit of a problem, but it's not a technical one. My problem is of a different nature, because I have just broken the news to my crew that I intend to stay with my ship. I have been trying unsuccessfully to persuade them all to return to the space station without me, but they are refusing to go. After a lengthy debate, we have decided to set a delay on the atomic governor so that we can move forward in time by at least one hundred years. We are all well aware of the dangers that might befall us but have jointly agreed that this is what we want to do".

Hans Zimmerman flew into a rage and demanded that they all return to the station immediately. Mike replied, "I'm sorry Mr. Zimmerman, but you're hardly in a position to be giving us orders now. Nevertheless, I should like to thank you and the professor for all the help you have given us. There is nothing more for me to say now other than to wish the remaining passengers and crew all the very best of luck with their new lives".

"Goodbye everyone!"

Suddenly there was an almighty bang from the rear end of the craft, followed by a blinding flash of white light that lit up the entire gallery. Once the light returned to normal, the spacecraft had simply disappeared. Both the professor and Hans Zimmerman stood gazing upwards with a look of shock and disbelief on their faces. After a few minutes, the professor composed himself and said, "It seems that Captain Morgan and his team have made the courageous decision to stay with their beloved spacecraft. Who knows where they might end up. I'm sure you will join me in wishing them good luck and pray that God will take care of them on their fateful voyage".

Epilogue

The year is 2180 on an international space traffic control station orbiting Mars. Ben Zimmerman, who is a junior controller, had just come on shift and was busy studying a hologram of the solar system, when he suddenly noticed something strange. He called for his team leader, saying, "Sir, you need to come and see this right now because an unidentified craft has just appeared out of nowhere in my sector, and it looks like it's heading this way.

THE END